SPORTS BIOGRAPHIES

PATRICK MAHOMES

KENNY ABDO

Fly!
An Imprint of Abdo Zoom
abdobooks.com

abdobooks.com

Published by Abdo Zoom, a division of ABDO, P.O. Box 398166, Minneapolis,
Minnesota 55439. Copyright © 2021 by Abdo Consulting Group, Inc. International
copyrights reserved in all countries. No part of this book may be reproduced in any
form without written permission from the publisher. Fly!™ is a trademark and logo
of Abdo Zoom.

052020
092020

THIS BOOK CONTAINS RECYCLED MATERIALS

Photo Credits: AP Images, Alamy, Icon Sportswire, iStock, newscom, Shutterstock
Production Contributors: Kenny Abdo, Jennie Forsberg, Grace Hansen
Design Contributors: Dorothy Toth, Neil Klinepier

Library of Congress Control Number: 2019956195

Publisher's Cataloging-in-Publication Data

Names: Abdo, Kenny, author.
Title: Patrick Mahomes / by Kenny Abdo
Description: Minneapolis, Minnesota : Abdo Zoom, 2021 | Series: Sports biographies |
    Includes online resources and index.
Identifiers: ISBN 9781098221409 (lib. bdg.) | ISBN 9781098222383 (ebook) |
    ISBN 9781098222871 (Read-to-Me ebook)
Subjects: LCSH: Mahomes, Patrick, 1995---Juvenile literature. | Professional athletes-
    United States--Biography--Juvenile literature. | Football players--United States--
    Biography--Juvenile literature. | Quarterbacks (Football)--Biography--Juvenile
    literature. | African American football players--Biography--Juvenile literature
Classification: DDC 796.332092 [B]--dc23

TABLE OF CONTENTS

PATRICK MAHOMES

Collecting trophies, awards, and records, Patrick Mahomes is a football-playing behemoth.

The starting **quarterback** for the Kansas City Chiefs has achieved greatness ever since his NFL **debut** in 2017.

EARLY YEARS

Patrick Lavon Mahomes was born in Tyler, Texas, in 1995.

Oklahoma

New Mexico

TYLER ■

Texas

Mexico

Mahomes played baseball all throughout high school. He was so good that the Detroit Tigers **drafted** him in 2014 right out of high school in the 37th round.

Mahomes went to Texas Tech instead of going pro. As **quarterback**, he smashed **NCAA** records and received the Sammy Baugh **trophy** for best college passer.

GOING PRO

The Kansas City Chiefs **drafted** Mahomes during first-round picks in 2017. Mahomes played his first game at starting **quarterback** in 2018 on September 9th. The Chiefs beat the LA Chargers 38-28.

Mahomes is the youngest player ever to complete six touchdown passes in one game. Playing against the Pittsburgh Steelers, he broke that record one day before his 23rd birthday.

Mahomes led the Chiefs to the 2018 AFC **Championship** game. This was something the team had not done since 1993. Unfortunately, the Chiefs lost to New England, 31-37.

Mahomes was named to the Pro Bowl in 2019. He threw an amazing 26 touchdowns, which earned him the offensive **MVP** award.

Mahomes and the Kansas City Chiefs won **Super Bowl** LIV. They defeated the San Francisco 49ers 31-20.

LEGACY

Mahomes is the youngest player to win the regular-season **MVP** and **Super Bowl** MVP awards, and take home a Super Bowl ring.

In 2019, Mahomes established the 15 and the Mahomies Foundation. The foundation's main focus is to improve the lives of less fortunate children.

GLOSSARY

championship – a game held to find a first-place winner.

debut – a first appearance.

draft – to select a professional athlete by a process and assign them to a certain team.

MVP – short for Most Valuable Player, in sports, an award given to the best-performing athlete.

NCAA – short for the National Collegiate Athletic Association, the governing body of most college sport competitions to make sure they are fair, safe, and sportsmanlike.

Super Bowl – the National Football League championship game, played annually between the champions of the National and the American Football Conferences.

ONLINE RESOURCES

Booklinks
NONFICTION NETWORK
FREE! ONLINE NONFICTION RESOURCES

To learn more about Patrick Mahomes, please visit **abdobooklinks.com** or scan this QR code. These links are routinely monitored and updated to provide the most current information available.

INDEX